Thunderstruck

By

Valerie Mann

Reviews for this book

Lightning-charged romance between a small-town teacher slash witch and the son of Thor. Thunder rolls and electricity crackles in this hot romance. Almost too hot for words...almost! ~ Romance Addict

Thunderstruck is set in the universe of supernatural beings. Witches? Check. Werewolves? Check. Mermaids? Check. Hot demigod? Checkity-check-check! ~ Amazon Reviewer

Between uncomfortable situations and bizarre weather changes, these two manage to realize there is more than thunder between them—there're also a lot of lightning-charged emotions! ~ Amazon Reviewer

Blurb

Between her part-time job as a preschool teacher for the local coven children, and proud new owner of the Blessed Bee bakery, Tamsin Riley has no time for anything but the occasional catnap and an organic power bar. Finding *The One* isn't on her radar, and that's perfectly fine. He'd never be able to keep up with her anyway.

As the illegitimate son of the thunder god Thor, Raiden Alexander has had his fair share of rejection, but never by the opposite sex. He likes the playboy lifestyle he's cultivated for the last hundred years or so, and the last thing he's interested in is settling down—unless it's between a beautiful woman's thighs. Becoming guardian of his four year-old nephew, Roman, puts a crimp in Raiden's love life, but he can handle temporary abstinence for the kid's sake. That is, until he meets Roman's teacher.

Sparks fly and thunder rolls each time Tamsin and Raiden come near each other. But how long before lightning finally strikes…and what happens then?

Dedication

To all the people who inspire me to write, push me to write, and ignore my whining when I can't write. But Tamsin and Raiden's story got told. I told you it would.

Chapter One

"The wolf huffed and he puffed...." I turned the page then spun the storybook around to let the students sitting on the floor at my feet view the colorful pictures. "But before he could blow the house down, the little piggy cast a Tolerance spell." I paused for dramatic effect. The kids loved it when magic intervened and foiled a nefarious plot.

A hand tapped my shoe. "And they all lived happily ever after?"

I glanced down at the wide-eyed little girl. "Well, Crimson—"

The boy beside her pulled her braid and laughed. "No, *stupid,* the pigs killed the wolf and ate him. Ow!" He jerked backward and rubbed his chest. "Miss Tamsin, she just zapped me!"

"Pull my hair again, and I'll make you wet your pants." Crimson shrugged. "*Stupid.*"

I loved my job. Teaching the bright, nimble minds of the children from the local coven community was definitely rewarding. But corralling fifteen inexperienced four-year-old witches each day was like herding cats. Their undeveloped powers tended to be so…uncontrolled.

"Crimson, please apologize to Roman." The poor boy's black hair haloed outward in inky spikes. I stifled a grin. She really *had* zapped him. "And, Roman, keep your hands to yourself."

Pretending not to notice my charges sticking their tongues out at each other, I lifted the picture book once again and raised my voice to a swinish squeal. *"Mr. Wolf, please don't blow our house down! Come inside, we have a lovely vegetable stew to share!"* Under the little pigs' spell, the wolf smiled a big, toothy grin, entered their house, and enjoyed a fine dinner with them. The end."

"Yay, harm no one!" Crimson clapped her hands. "They used their magic for good!"

Roman rolled his eyes and crossed his pudgy arms. "My uncle says the best wolf is a dead wolf."

Crimson's lower lip trembled, and she promptly burst into tears. Not that it stopped her from considering retaliation, and when her hand fluttered in his direction, Roman edged away, obviously anticipating another jolt.

Every day, he parroted his uncle. *My uncle thinks this, my uncle said that.* I'd decided I didn't like the man very much and couldn't wait until the looming Meet-the-Parents Night with Roman's mother and father so I could discuss the questionable influence their relative had on their impressionable son.

A few minutes later, I tidied up the classroom while my assistant, Katarina, supervised the children on the small playground outside. A sniffle from the doorway caught my attention.

Crimson hugged the frame, her face blotchy and wet with tears. "Miss Tamsin, are wolves bad?" She dragged an arm across her eyes.

I saw the direction she was headed in and had to tread carefully. I wasn't a big fan of dogs of any species. Cats suit my kind. However, I also hated the doubt shimmering in her eyes. Waving her over, I yanked a tissue out of the supersize box on my desk and wiped her nose.

"No, sweetie. Wolves aren't bad."

She didn't appear convinced. "If wolves are bad, that means my daddy is bad."

I knelt down and hugged her. "Your father is a wonderful man who loves you very much." *Even if he is long in the tooth and has hair sprouting out of his ears.* Luckily, Crimson had inherited her mother's fine-boned, elegant, witchy features, rather than her hirsute father's werewolf DNA.

She sniffed again. "Roman says his uncle likes to eat wolves with ketchup."

I bit my tongue. And could not *wait* for the parent-teacher conference to happen.

***

Two evenings later, I prepared for the first Meet-the-Parents Night of the year. As the hour approached, I grew impatient and distracted. I always enjoyed getting to know the families in our fast-growing coven, but the normal banter and rowdiness of the fifteen four-year-olds made me antsy and by the time they'd filed out to the carpool to go home, I wanted to jump out of my skin.

Katarina paused in the middle of erasing the whiteboard. "Are you okay, Tamsin?"

I couldn't explain why I jerked at every sharp noise or quick movement. Or why the hair on my neck stood at attention each time I glanced at the clock. Sensations of excitement and dread warred with one another in my belly until I was forced to dig into the bottom of my purse for an ancient roll of antacid tablets. After brushing away the lint stuck to them, I popped a couple, chewed, and grimaced.

Running a hand across my nape to make the hairs stand down, I shrugged. "I'm always anxious meeting parents for the first time."

"It's going to be an interesting night, for sure." She tossed the eraser in a small basket hanging on a hook near the board. "I'll see you at the bakery tomorrow morning. Don't forget, we have that ginormous carrot-flaxseed muffin order for the coven meeting. And I'll make sure there's a double espresso waiting for you." With a wink, she slung a huge leather bag over one shoulder and headed for the door. "'Cause, yeah…you're going to need it after tonight."

"Wait!" When she paused, I asked, "What are you not telling me?"

Katarina, a half-breed, but still blessed with a healthy bit of clairvoyance, grinned. "I can't tell you. But, man, I wish I could stay and watch."

"Watch what?" I practically yelped. And why wasn't I seeing what *she* was seeing?

"Laters." With a wave, she shot out the door.

Make that an annoying bit of clairvoyance.

My stomach churned then, furry antacids or not, and when the appointments were nearly over, anxiety had crawled over my skin and worn me out. One mom and dad remained on my list—Roman's parents—before I could go home.

I stared at the doorway. Perspiration bloomed, and I rubbed sweaty palms on my slacks. After straightening the chairs in the classroom for the hundredth time, I alphabetized the picture books on the shelf and nipped a dead leaf off the spider plant sitting in a gaudy, beaded pot made by one of my very first students.

My heart started to thud erratically, my ears rang, and I sat down hard in one of the little-people chairs nearby before the floor and I became more intimately acquainted. *Goddess! What is wrong with me?* I swept a palm over my forehead and tried to control the hyperventilation by convincing myself one of the children had infected me with a bug.

Really. Who was I kidding?

Katarina may be a decent precog, but I'm better. And this was no bug. I might not know what was coming, but I doubted a double espresso would take care of its aftereffects.

A sudden gust of wind battered the tall windows overlooking the playground, and rain pelted the glass. I wondered if I'd remembered to close my car windows, but doubted it, since the weather forecast had predicted nothing but clear autumn weather. The rain hammered harder, and nausea roiled in my gut. Breathing through my mouth, I grabbed Roman's student folder sitting nearby and fanned my face.

Just when I thought it might be a good idea to put my head between my knees, the door swung open. Lifting my head, I found a lone, dark figure filling the entrance. Lightning flashed so intense, black spots dotted my vision. And, goddess, was I suddenly glad the floor wasn't too far away. Maybe I'd only suffer some bruises when I bounced off it in a dead faint.

Because whoever stood there was *not* Roman's parents.

Chapter Two

A thunderous crack rent the room, and the air shimmered and waved. I clutched my chest in a bid for breath, and with a relieved gasp, sucked oxygen.

"Well, shit." The voice—deep, masculine, and sounding more than a little annoyed—drifted to me while residual echoes of the man's noisy entrance zigzagged off the walls.

Still a little breathless, I leaned back in the kiddie seat and met the piercing eyes of the most compelling man I'd ever seen. Ink-black hair fell to his shoulders and, dressed in black from head to toe, he wore a scowl as dark as his clothes.

Desire, hot and thick, slammed between us, and—oh, not again—stole my breath. Unbidden, hazy snippets of future events—the kind every teenage witch dreamt of and her father guarded against—engulfed me.

He's the one.

I had no idea who he was or why he stood in my

9

classroom, but, for better or worse, my life would be forever entwined with his.

Clearing my throat, I stood on watery legs and pushed the chair under its desk, grasping the folder in one hand while keeping a grip for support on the backrest with the other. "Can I help you?" *Hallelujah.* My voice sounded normal even with my heart in near-arrhythmia.

"Tamsin Riley?"

I frowned. I'd been Miss Tamsin for so long, I couldn't remember the last time I'd heard my surname used in the classroom. Probably never. Meeting his gaze again, I nodded.

He's the one. The only *one.*

His presence, even larger than the man himself, consumed the space with immense power. "I'm Raiden Alexsander."

His name meant nothing to me, so I dug into his mind to get an ID on him, a breach of etiquette and privacy, not to mention socially unacceptable. If any of my students tried it, I'd put them in time out for, like, forever. Then call their parents.

Whatever.

I'm not four years old, and rather than expose my ignorance to *The One*, I didn't hesitate to dive into his gorgeous head. Raising one brow, Raiden effectively blocked the invasion, letting me know how he felt about it. More lightning flashed, rocking thunder right behind it, and the overhead fluorescent lights flickered and burst, raining shards of glass in a tinkling melody over my head and shoulders. While I shrieked and ducked, it didn't pass my notice that not one sliver landed on him.

The mental wall I hit was so solid, I reeled, barely staying upright. But right before he'd shut me out, I'd seen something. Something he wouldn't want me to see. Something my dad most definitely wouldn't want anyone to see, especially his daughter.

The earlier nausea returned twofold, until my mouth watered. With a convulsive one-two swallow, I crossed my arms and reconsidered the sit-down, head-between-the-knees thing.

It can't be, can't be, can't be. The singsong chant filled my mind and helped me work past the upchuck idea and through the whole world-altering knowledge that Mr. Right had finally made an appearance…on Meet-the-Parents Night. And wasn't that the story of my life…bad timing always knew where to find me.

Steeling my spine, I met his stone-cold stare. "Mr. Alexsander—"

He lounged against the doorjamb, arms crossed, the very picture of insolence. Like he didn't give a damn my life had just taken a turn I wasn't ready to deal with. I'm way too busy for Mr. Right, Mr. Right Now, or even Mr. Next Decade.

"I thought you'd be different."

"Excuse me?" To buy some time and collect myself, I opened Roman's student folder and flipped through the progress report and notes and colorful pictures, the papers stiff from fragrant finger paint. Glancing past whoever this guy was, I strained to hear any movement out in the hallway. Where *were* Roman's parents? I needed a lifeline.

"A schoolteacher." Looking me up and down, Raiden Alexsander shrugged. "Never saw *that* coming."

Oh no, he did not *just say. ..* The arrogant dickhead. When my soul mate finaly showed up, the last thing I wanted to hear was how disappointing he found me. Putting my back to him, I crossed the room, the glass crunching under my feet—I'd have to stay late to vacuum the mess, thank you very much— and slapped Roman's file on my desk. My Irish temper rose, and my hands shook.

Without turning, I asked, "I'm sorry, but who are you?"

"You know who I am."

Peeking over my shoulder, I watched him straighten; oozing sensual promise from every pore, flooding my body with anticipation for what he had in store for me. Regardless, he remained a dickhead.

Another crack of thunder rattled the windows and monsoon-like winds battered the building.

"Mr. Alexsander—"

"Raiden." He smirked. "We may as well be on a first-name basis, after all."

Hmmm. *I don't think so,* said my brain. *Hell yeah,* said my body. A thrill of fear and arousal shafted through me.

"Actually, *Mr. Alexsander*, I really don't know who you are. But, if you'll excuse me, I'm waiting for—"

One moment, he stood across the room, the next, he leaned so close behind me, his breath brushed my cheek. "I'm the one you've been waiting for."

Ignoring the little somersault my tummy did at his nearness, I angled my head around to stare at his mouth—it was nearly level with mine, after all. Lickable, full lips, framed by a sexy five o'clock shadow I wanted to scrape my nails across to hear the rasp. I swayed against him as if pulled by an invisible wire.

Swallowing past the lump in my throat, I said, "You need to leave. I'm waiting for the parents of one of my students." I made a show of looking at my watch; the watch that wasn't there since I usually used my cell phone to tell time. Feeling foolish, I shifted my gaze to the clock over the door. "They should be here any minute."

He quirked an eyebrow. "Roman's parents, you

mean."

It wasn't a question, and how had he known which kid's parents were due? A shimmer of unease rippled over me as my precog power filled in the blanks. A little late for it to finally kick in. Epic superpower fail. But, evidently, Roman's mother and father were not on their way.

They'd sent the uncle.

Roman's bad influence.

The one who liked werewolves with ketchup.

The One.

Chapter Three

Control. *Must get control.* Because it was obvious if I didn't, the bad-influence, ketchup-loving, hot-as-sin uncle would steamroll right over me. *Not going to happen.*

Gesturing toward the squat little chair beside him, I said, "Have a seat, Mr. Alexsander."

He swung it out from under the table and frowned down at it. "Do you have anything a bit more...grown-up?"

I crossed my arms. "Maybe you were too busy shattering light bulbs and monsooning the parking lot to notice, but this is a preschool classroom." Actually, I could have offered him one of the two larger chairs tucked behind my desk, but I wanted him in a position of subordination. The kind involving knees wedged under the chin.

Settling on the hard plastic, he managed to look both enormous and comfortable, damn it. I opened Roman's folder and sat on the edge of the table rather than join Raiden on a neighboring seat, and forced him to look up at me. Black eyes, unfathomably deep and full of secrets, met mine.

He rested an arm on the table, nearly touching my leg. I glared pointedly at it. He didn't move. "Roman has told me about you, Tamsin."

Normally, a statement like that would be followed by something like, *only good things, of course*, or, *it's a pleasure to finally meet you*. Apparently, Roman's uncle didn't believe in pesky add-ons, because the statement hung in the air, allowing me to draw unwelcome conclusions. Temper bubbled in my gut, along with defensiveness.

Stay in control.

"Can I ask where Roman's parents are?" I eased my leg an inch away from his long, tanned finger.

The corner of Raiden's upper lip twitched in derision. "They're on sabbatical in Scotland. Roman's father is doing that damned Druid research he's so obsessed with, you know."

Druid? No, I didn't know. But Raiden obviously found it a useless course of study, at the very least.

"And they'll be back when?"

"My sister will be back before the winter solstice. If we're all very lucky, she'll come home alone."

Ah…no love lost between the brothers-in-law. I wondered what that was about. Then again, Mr. Crankypants probably didn't get along with too many people.

Raiden tilted his head to the side and frowned up at me. "I'm Roman's guardian for the time being. Let's get this meeting over with, shall we?" He yanked another short chair from under the table. "Sit."

And lose my advantage perch? Not a chance. "Thank you, but I prefer to stay where I am."

Narrowing his eyes, he eased upward, bits of glass snapping under his feet, until he towered over me and totally invaded my personal space. Witches tend to get a little threatened by that, given how badly they've been treated over the centuries, and it was all I could do not to cower. Distrust runs thick with strangers. And that's the only reason why I wanted to cower.

Really.

He flattened his palms on either side of my hips. His eyes, a midnight blue—not black as I'd thought—and framed with short, thick lashes, held my own. "Then we shall conduct the meeting here."

"Mr. Alexsander, I—"

A finger touched my lips, as if to shush me, but I jerked and gasped. The slight contact had shot a bolt of electricity straight to my core. Thunder grumbled in the distance. Raiden's eyes narrowed again. And he smirked.

"My mother told me you would respond to my touch that way. She was right."

"Your mother doesn't know me," I managed to whisper. And I didn't think I wanted to know his mother if she was anything like her son.

"She knows all about you." His finger caressed my cheek, and I shivered. "She has told me many things." His gaze never left my lips. I stared at his and wondered what they'd feel like. Hard and brutal? Soft and gentle?

I'll take hard and brutal for one thousand, Alex.

Curiosity…goddess, it has gotten me into more trouble in my twenty-five years, but that didn't stop me…. "What else did she tell you?" I breathed.

"That you will never be satisfied."

Recalling the things I'd seen before Raiden had shut me out of his mind made me tremble. The thunder warned again. "Never satisfied with what?"

"This." He pressed his lips against mine.

A jagged flash of light and a sound, like the crack of a whip, filled the room and the same electric current I'd felt a moment earlier arced from my lips to my clit. An orgasm hit hard and fast, and I jolted, feeling my ass slide toward the edge of the table. Then it was over. The shortest, most amazing release. If it hadn't been so awesome, I might have been a little annoyed.

Wait—I *was* annoyed. Especially when Raiden chuckled. My eyes popped open, and a warm flush of humiliation crept up my neck when I realized he didn't appear aroused in the slightest, only amused by my response to his kiss.

He ran a hand up my back, and little waves of

energy followed its path. Not unpleasant, but disconcerting since I feared they'd set off another....

Control. He took it, Tamsin. Get it back.

"Your mother sounds like an interesting woman." At some point during my mini-orgasm, I'd opened my legs enough to let him stand between them. Rubbing the sole of one shoe up the back of his leg, I tilted my head and licked my lower lip. "There is one thing I don't think she mentioned though."

Ah, finally—the arousal I'd been waiting for. His pupils dilated and he flared his nostrils, his attention fixed on my mouth. "Like what?"

"This." Lifting my hands, I laid them over his rock-hard pectorals and hit him with all the power I possessed. Seconds later, I crunched my way across the room and leaned down to offer him a hand. Slouched against the wall, he ignored my friendly gesture and rubbed the back of his head, having landed under a sign with the classroom's simple motto: *Harm No One*.

Oops.

Chapter Four

The sun hadn't bothered to crest the horizon before I pulled into the alley behind the bakery. After parking next to Katarina's ancient VW bug, Eloise, I juggled a box of carrots and huge burlap bag of fresh parsley under one arm and wet beach towels under the other. I kicked the base of the kitchen's back door to get Kat's attention.

She flipped the dead bolt and held the door wide to let me in. The heavenly aroma of fresh-baked bread filled the room. Asking her to open the shop that morning instead of me had been a stroke of genius. Although it wasn't like I'd slept a wink since The One's sudden intrusion into my orderly life, so I guess I could have opened and let Kat sleep an extra few hours.

Snagging the carrots, she set them on a worktable nearby then went to reach for the towels. She pulled her hand away with a grimace. "Do I even want to ask?"

22

I tossed them in a sodden heap on the nearby employee bathroom floor. "I left my car windows down yesterday and that biblical rainstorm last night flooded the interior. I'll probably be sitting on towels for days to avoid a wet ass." After donning an apron, I dumped the carrots into one of the sinks, began to scrub them, and griped, "Not to mention, my car smells like a wet dog."

The timer on the oven dinged, and Katarina pulled a dozen loaves of dark rye out and set them on a nearby rack. "Merlin can't help it that he loves to go for rides with Auntie Tamsin."

"One ride. And his mother never told Auntie Tamsin that Merlin gets carsick." That had been the first and last time I'd offered to dog-sit her stinky, motion-challenged basset hound. Not to mention, that weekend he'd terrorized my cat, Salem, to the point I'd been forced to research calming spells for felines. Those are not easy to find.

Taking a large grater and cutting board from under the table, Kat started shredding the carrots I'd handed her. She paused. "Wait a minute...we didn't have any rain last night."

I turned off the tap and, after gathering the remaining carrots, dropped them beside the board. "Where were you, in a different time zone? I don't know how you could've missed it."

She scooped the growing mound of carrot shavings into a bowl. "We didn't get any rain. In fact, I had to water my garden before leaving this morning. My spinach was beginning to wilt."

"That's impossible." The hair on my nape rose. When she didn't respond, I glanced up from the parsley I'd been chopping. Her smirk made the hair rise higher. "What."

She reached for something from the counter behind her. "I forgot to give this to you. Extra half-and-half, no sugar." Sliding a huge take-out cup of coffee toward me, she said, "I made it a triple shot. I had a feeling a double espresso wouldn't be enough."

The thick aromas of fresh coffee, grassy parsley, and pungent root vegetables didn't calm me. That didn't stop me from reaching for the cup though. I sighed with the first hit of the creamy brew. "Not enough for what?"

"Dealing with your new man. He's a hottie, by the way."

The coffee threatened to curdle in my stomach. Setting the cup nearby, I attacked the parsley with renewed vigor. "Don't know what you're talking about."

She snorted. "Uh huh."

Oh, hell, why bother with pretense? Kat had known about Crankypant's arrival long before I had. I pointed the knife in her direction and said, "For one thing, this is none of your business. For another, how the heck are you seeing things that I can't see? You're a half-breed."

Taking no offense, she said, "The correct term is bi-breed. And you're not supposed to see this coming. You know as well as I do that seeing your own future can have negative eternal repercussions." She smirked again. "Might not happen often, but it sucks when I'm better at foreseeing things than you, doesn't it?"

More like aggravating, especially when it

concerned *me*. Nevertheless.... "Spill it, Kat. Tell me what you know."

She wiped orange-stained hands on the towel tucked in her apron strings. Biting her upper lip, she didn't speak for a while. Up went the hairs on my neck again.

"Look, Tamsin, it's not a good idea—" Her high-pitched squawk split the air when I slammed my palm on the metal table.

"Tell me!" The man of my fantasies had shown up unexpectedly, which pissed me off because I hate surprises. The arrogant *hottie* had made me come with barely a touch, which I'd loved, but resented at the same time. And I'd barely slept a wink as a result. I was exhausted and crabby.

Her chin wobbled. *Great*. She had to be one of the most emotional half-breeds—*bi-breeds*—I'd ever met.

Guilt settled over me. "I'm sorry."

She sniffed and shrugged. "Fine. You really want to hear this?" Stalking to the walk-in, she yanked a cardboard tray of eggs out then began to crack them in rapid succession into the bowl of grated carrots. "He knows you're the one, but he thinks he's better than you." *Crack.*

"Tell me something I don't know." The jerk had made his opinion of my teacher status pretty clear.

"He'll get over it. He wants you too badly not to." *Crack.* "Grab that bag of sugar on the shelf for me." After I'd obeyed, she added, "By the way, he didn't sleep well last night either." I hadn't mentioned my insomnia, but maybe I looked as worn out as I felt. Her eyes met mine. "And he has a headache."

Bouncing off a concrete block wall could do that to a guy. *Natch.*

"Anything else?" Surely there was more. I mean, if he was my mate, there had to be.

"He's not the mama's boy you think he is, regardless of what he said. He knows what he wants, and he always gets it."

"Ah, so he's selfish *and* spoiled."

Kat ignored my comment then stopped blending the carrot-egg mixture to look up at the ceiling, as if recalling more information about my eternal repercussions. "And what happened last night is just the tip of the iceberg. He thinks he'll never be able to satisfy you, but he'll never stop trying."

Shit. What *didn't* my business partner know? My face heated at the thought she may have seen *everything* that had gone on with Raiden Alexsander and I.

"Anything else?" I asked again, hoping the sarcastic tone hid my mortification.

She gave the goopy mixture another couple of turns with the spatula. "Only that he's the son of a god."

Blink.

Blink.

"Excuse me?"

Rinsing her hands in the sink, she wiped them on her apron. "Well, he's actually a demigod since his mother isn't a god. She's a witch." Reaching under the worktable, Kat pulled out a crate of lemons and slid it toward me. Then snickered. "Goddess, I love it when you're speechless. Can you zest these?"

God? Demigod? What the ever-loving hell was

she talking about?

Like an automaton, I zested. Speechlessly. After the third scraped knuckle, I woke up enough to say, "Gods don't exist."

"Um, yeah, they do."

"Um, no they don't. They're mythological. Nobody believes they exist anymore, if they ever even did." I wound a Band-Aid around my index finger, pulled on a vinyl glove, and went back to zesting.

"So, you're saying they can't exist. In case you've forgotten, some people think we don't exist either. But you're a witch, I'm a witch—"

"Only half. And both of your halves are pissing me off right now."

Her eyes narrowed. "Let me get this straight— you teach a class of little witches, one of whom has a werewolf daddy, and another with a mermaid mommy. Because that's not weird at all." Kat added ground flaxseeds to the bowl and stirred. "But gods can't exist?"

Scooping the fragrant zest into the batter, I

shrugged, afraid if I said anything else, she'd start getting all misty-eyed again.

We worked wordlessly after that, mixing wet and dry ingredients then filling muffin tins with enough carrot flaxseed batter to feed a small coven, or large army. One thing can be said about witches: they do love their sweets. Especially when the treats are disguised as healthy.

After setting the timer on the oven, Kat sighed. "I'll clean up and start on the brownies and shortbread. Also, Zak Criss called and asked for another dozen lime tartlets. Selma is having cravings again."

I grabbed my coffee cup and headed through the swinging door leading to the sales floor. "Double the order. She's eating for three."

Staring at the row of coffee urns, I debated whether to fill the cup with more of Kat's high-octane brew, go decaf, or switch to green tea. My stomach hadn't settled after the first cup of espresso, but a long day loomed. I continued to obsess for a full minute or two, as though the beverage decision had life-altering consequences. I must have been tired if I couldn't make a choice.

Something tapped on the storefront windows. Forgetting about the drink, I turned toward the sound; rain, with the wind behind it, letting it find its way under the awnings to hit the glass. Circling around the display cases, I unlocked the door and stuck my head outside. The sun's faint rays glimmered on the horizon, but a thunderhead sat directly above Main Street.

My stomach rolled then, and I shivered. Like déjà vu all over again. Glancing up and down the street, I wasn't surprised to see two figures, adult and child, approaching. My body had already figured out what my failing superpowers hadn't. Through the downpour, Mr. Crankypants and his nephew were headed my way. Neither had a drop of moisture on them.

Roman broke away and skipped toward me. "Miss Tamsin!" Skidding to a halt, he grinned. "Uncle Raiden is in a bad mood. He said he had a rough night and needed coffee and revenge. Do you sell revenge?"

I raised an eyebrow at the sweet, and so innocent, little boy. "Oh, yes. I serve the best revenge in town."

Roman spun to stare up at Raiden, who'd stopped a yard or so behind him. "See? I told you she'd have some!"

My eyes met Raiden's over his nephew's head. Anger and sensual promise stared back at me while thunder growled in warning. *Are we going to do this again?* As if hearing my thoughts, the dickhead nodded.

Roman pushed past me and into the shop. Standing in front of the display case, he pressed his nose against the glass. "I want one of those," he said, pointing at a half-moon cookie the size of his head. "And a chocolate cupcake with those green sprinkles."

"Not the healthiest way to start the day, honey." I slipped back behind the case and pulled out one of Blessed Bee's famous breakfast cookies. "This would be a better choice."

Clearly less than impressed, he poked at the

hearty brown cookie and sniffed it. "Is this what revenge smells like?"

Raiden laid a large tanned hand on Roman's head. "She only serves that to grownups." Our gazes met again, and locked. "Right, *Miss Tamsin?*"

I glared. Goddess, this schoolteacher-slash-bakery-owner wanted to put him in his place. My exhaustion foiled that desire. "That's correct. Would you like some?" Well, hell, that hadn't come out right. I'd just given him what he'd come for, permission to have revenge.

"More than you know." He grinned.

And I discovered the meaning of swoon.

Oh, sweet goddess, no romance novel in the world had ever adequately defined the knee-buckling, heart-palpitating sensation. And as my belly went into freefall and squeezed the breath out of my lungs, Raiden did me one more favor, granting me a vision of how he planned to exact his revenge. The image of sweaty, tangled, naked limbs vanished almost before I could process it, but something odd stood out: it had been snowing.

Evidently, he took the old saying literally: *revenge is a dish best served cold.*

Chapter Five

"We aren't officially open yet. But here." I filled a to-go cup with Kat's highest-octane brew, adding a cardboard sleeve to it out of habit, not because I cared whether dickhead burned his hand on the scalding coffee.

"Are you trying to get rid of us, Miss Tamsin?" The corner of Raiden's mouth lifted in a hint of a smile.

He's really enjoying this.

"She's too nice to kick us out," Roman said, giving the breakfast cookie a tentative lick.

"Actually, I have a lot left to do before we can serve customers." I glanced at the clock on the microwave. "Less than fifteen minutes from now, in fact." I seriously hoped his uncle took the hint and beat feet out of the shop. Customers be damned, I needed every one of those fifteen minutes to bring my heart back into a regular rhythm.

"I think that's our cue to leave, sport." Raiden

patted him on the shoulder. Then, digging a wallet out of his rear pants pocket, he pulled out a credit card and handed it to me. I didn't want to take his money, but he also didn't strike me as the type of guy who would let me comp him some caffeine and a snack either. I slid the credit slip across the counter for him to sign, noting he was both left-handed and had the most interesting script. Very blocky, each letter precise, almost like a printer had printed it, not his hand.

Raiden wordlessly separated the original and copy, handed one to me.

Roman wiggled beside him, stabbing a pudgy finger at the glass case he had his nose pressed to. He lifted his midnight-blue eyes to meet mine. I'd never noticed their color before. Exactly like his uncle's. "Maybe we can come back later and get that?" he asked with longing, pointing at the half-moon cookie.

"Oh, we'll be back," Raiden assured him.

Our gazes clashed, his daring...daring what, I wasn't sure, but I had no doubt he'd let me know. *Hopefully it involves sweaty, naked, tangled limbs,* said my libido. And again, as if hearing my thoughts, Raiden dipped his head and smiled, accompanied by a gust of wind battering the canvas awning, and the supports creaking in protest.

Before I lost my entire storefront, I stepped out of the lusty aura surrounding us and knelt to give Roman a hug. "I'm going to set that cookie aside. When you come back, you can have it, but only if your uncle reports you ate a healthy lunch."

Roman clung to me, skinny arms hooked around my neck for several moments, and I had the distinct impression, although living with his cool Uncle Raiden was buckets of fun, he missed his mom. "Thanks, Miss Tamsin." He pulled back. "Can you put some of those green sprinkles on it?"

A strong, tanned hand rested on the boy's head. "Don't press your luck, little man."

"He can't help it," I snapped. "Apparently, it's hereditary."

Raiden chuckled, so quietly I nearly missed it, but I got a little swoony nevertheless. "Perhaps." Without another word, he guided his charge out the door.

I watched them until they were out of sight.

***

By midmorning, Blessed Bee had sold out of nearly every breakfast pastry and a few gallons of tea and coffee, I'd found my second wind, and I was ready to open the other side of the shop, Bob Barkery. Catering to our four-legged customers, and only open on Saturdays, the pet bakery had heavy paw traffic, and not surprisingly, a very cheerful clientele.

Katarina, the town's most notable animal lover and rescuer, had purchased the empty video store next to Blessed Bee, then pulled some serious waterworks until she'd convinced me that knocking out the wall between the two spaces and opening a pet treat bakery was the best idea since...well, *ever*. Secretly, I'd loved the idea from the start. I simply let her blubber for a while because she was so cute when she did.

Separated by a dutch door, customers in both

shops didn't mingle due to local health laws. Not that the door's lower half kept Blessed Bee's curious two-legged variety from hanging over the edge and admiring the furry ones. And I'd no sooner locked the bottom half behind me and unlocked Bob Barkery's front door, when a short chorus of canned barking, a campy version of a doorbell, announced our first customer of the day.

Ricardo Solis shuffled in behind his pretty greyhound, Maia. Rescued from a dog track less than a year earlier, she'd been shy and introverted. No longer. Showing every pearly tooth, she grinned and danced near the glass case holding her favorite snacks.

"Hey, Ric. Maia taking you for a walk today?" I asked, while bagging a few of the cat-shaped cheddar-bacon cookies she adored. I threw in handful of peanut butter-parsley bites as a bonus.

He wiped sweat from his forehead. "As usual." Tugging Maia's leash to pull her away from a rack of hemp dog collars for sale, he added, "So, is...uh...Katarina around?"

Pretending to look for something, I bent behind the register and grinned. Would the guy ever get the nerve to ask Kat out? He and my business partner had enough in common to have even Dr. Phil give a blessing upon their union. Both half—er—bi-breeds, they shared a love of animals, organic-everything, bluegrass music, and for crying out loud, even wore the same tired black Birkenstocks, circa 1990.

Straightening, I nodded. "She's in the back. Let me fetch her for you."

Ric waved his hands to protest, dropping Maia's leash. Seeing her advantage, the hound bolted in the small space, one gangly leg catching the base of the collar rack, sending it crashing into a shelf with hand-thrown clay cookie jars. Ric shouted, and Maia yelped then bounced in and out of the communal water bowl near the door to sail for parts unknown. I had no clue where, since I was too busy watching the jars, and my profit margin for the day, tumble toward the floor. A split-second later, they slowed and settled gently on the tile, with only a slight rattle of their lids.

The door between the bakeries swung open and

Kat stood, hands on hips, to survey the chaos. "Seriously...what would you do without me?"

Thanks to Kat's handy intervention, the mess had been minimal, so after a red-faced Ricardo helped clean up, in between making puppy-eyes at Kat and giving Maia some good-natured scolding, Bob Barkery was back in business with nary a scratch.

I'd just finished wiping Maia's wet paw prints off the countertop when the front door barked. The Mercedes-Benz of all strollers rolled in, carrying a pink, gurgling bundle of baby, followed by beaming parents and a precious puppy straining to get past them.

Giving the counter one last swipe, I threw the paper towel in the trash and came around to greet the happy family. "Rowena! It's so nice to see you out and about!" I gave her a hug and one to the handsome man standing beside her. "Hello, Caine."

His piercing blue eyes met mine. "Hi, Tamsin. Rocky needs some treats."

On cue, the plump English Bulldog pup jumped

up on the footrest of the stroller for attention then tumbled off again. With a bark of clueless joy, he scrambled toward Maia, only to be stopped cold when he ran out of leash. Sitting back on his plump backside, he whined.

I crouched in front of the stroller. "Oh my! Opal's getting so big!" The pretty baby, wrapped up against the autumn chill in a fuzzy pink-and-yellow blanket so only her face showed, stared at me with the same, intense blue eyes as her dad's and gave a cavernous yawn. Reaching in, I wiggled what I assumed was a foot through the bulky covering. "Hi, sweetie." And after a solemn assessment, she blew a bubble and grinned in return.

I straightened and waved toward the glass cases. "Come on over. Let's get Rocky a snack."

Rowena followed me over to the counter, with the puppy tagging along. As I grabbed a wax paper bag, she leaned in close, playing with the crystal she always wore around her neck. "We aren't really here for treats."

Pausing, I raised an eyebrow. "Oh?" And why

didn't that surprise me? Rowena had always been the caretaker in our tight circle of friends.

She reached into the pocket of her sweater jacket and pulled out a small, tissue paper-wrapped object. "Here. You're going to need this."

Curious, I took it. Whatever was inside glowed yellow, and emitted considerable warmth. Maybe even vibrated. I knew then it had to be a crystal. Carefully opening the package, I found not one, but two small stones, and a leather drawstring pouch.

"Black tourmaline and citrine," Rowena said. "I couldn't decide which you needed more, so brought both. I would have come by sooner, but they had to be cleansed first, and with the baby and all...."

I didn't know what to say. Row used crystals for all types of reasons: healing, protection, love, health...but she'd never given me one. Well, we never discussed the time I'd begged her to give me a crystal to entice Bradley Dale to ask me to the solstice party, back when we'd been freshmen in high school. Her skills hadn't been sufficiently developed, evidently, and neither had mine, or I would have cooked up a love potion or conjured a spell. Regardless of our mutual ineptitude, *something* worked because Brad had ended up asking every girl in our class *but* me to the party. They'd all said yes, of course. Who wouldn't have said yes to the gorgeous Bradley Dale back then? The ensuing chaos when they'd all found out about each other was legendary. People still talked about it. Except Row and I, of course.

"Um...thank you. But why do you think I need these?" They were so lovely, but I had no clue what to do with them.

Plucking them from my palm, she shoved them in the pouch and stuffed it in the breast pocket of my apron. Warmth and that weird vibration weighted against my sternum in a rather nice way. Calming, actually.

"You need to have powers of discernment, but also open-mindedness." Her gaze darted restlessly around the small room. "And lots and lots of protection until you figure things out."

I frowned. "Are you okay?"

"I...." She fanned her suddenly flushed face. "Is it

hot in here?"

It didn't feel uncomfortably warm to me. Maybe she was coming down with some bug. Goddess knew what critters she might have picked up at all of the play dates she took Opal to. The baby already had a busy social calendar.

The door barked, thunder cracked, and poor Rowena jumped like she'd spotted a snake. Rocky and Maia yipped with apparent delight while Caine tried to move the super-deluxe stroller out of the way to let the new arrivals inside the increasingly tight space. I didn't have to see around Caine's tall body to know who'd made such a grand entrance.

Rowena let out a little squeak and clutched the crystal around her neck. "I got here in the nick of time." Her husband crouched to comfort Opal, who'd begun to squall at the sudden commotion.

Raiden stood in the entrance, staring at me, his eyes filled with...what? Lust, anger, desire...need? *Caution!* warned the crystals between my suddenly perky girls.

Walking backward at an odd angle, Roman tried

to push his way around his uncle and into the shop. "Come on, Gunnar!" Struggling with something, he finally popped into the crowded room, tugging a portly puppy in with him. Looking worn out, the poor dog planted his butt firmly on the tile and began to pant.

Rocky went ballistic, forgetting the leash anchoring him to Rowena's wrist, and flew full-bore toward the new canine, nearly strangling himself when the end of the lead stopped him short. It made no dent in his enthusiasm to reach the other pup, and it was clear why: they were obviously siblings, in all of their adorable, identical rotundness. Gunnar barked a greeting and tripped over his paws to get to his brother. Happily re-bonding, they rolled on the floor, gnawed each other's ears, and growled.

An odd roaring began in my ears.

Roman tugged on my sleeve. "We came back for my cookie, and Gunnar needs some, too."

Giving myself a stern mental shake, I tried to force attention away from the compelling man who currently dominated Bob Barkery with an eerie force, and focus instead on his nephew.

Instead, all I truly noticed was Raiden, stock-still in the doorway, and everything and everyone else moving in slow motion, as though time had begun to flow at a different speed for everyone but us. Noise and chatter had been reduced to a muffle as though I'd pressed my head against a pillow. And the crystals tag-teaming in my pocket twitched, like they knew they were way out of their league to help me.

It had to be the weirdest thing I'd ever experienced.

Raiden lifted his chin, gestured to the others around us, and said in a crystal-clear voice, "Get rid of these people."

His rudeness angered and horrified me. None of the adults but Kat, and possibly Rowena, had a clue who he was. What would my friends and customers think, hearing a stranger asking me to tell them to leave?

"Excuse me?" I glanced around the room. Nobody seemed to have heard Raiden's command. Rowena lifted a red-faced and teary Opal out of her seat at the speed of snail, patting her back in a soothing gesture that couldn't have topped three pats per minute. The puppies rolled over my toes in a chunky little ball, their jaws moving with what must have been barks of joy, but I heard only odd chirping. Maia reared on her hind legs with a comical slo-mo bark while eyeing the commotion, with Ricardo straining to keep her steady.

Meeting Raiden's eyes, I narrowed mine. *Goddess!* What sorcery was this? None I'd ever encountered, for real.

He lifted an imperious brow, obviously impatient. "You heard me. We need to talk. Make these people leave."

"I don't think so." *Dickhead*, I almost added. "I'm not interested in anyth—"

"Oh, for the love of Odin, I'll do it," he snapped.

And the space-time continuum was restored. Movement in the store returned to normal, Opal squalled heartily, dogs yipped, Roman was trying to climb over the shelf of the locked Dutch door to get at his cookie in the people bakery, and Kat and Ricardo were making their usual goo-goo eyes at each other. The door barked open and within seconds, each of my customers, except Roman and Kat, made their good-byes and started to file out, clueless they were being manipulated.

I couldn't help it; my jaw dropped. I could *not* believe what Raiden had just done, and even if he gave me roses, financial security, and earth-shattering orgasms every day for the rest of my life, I didn't trust him or like him one bit. Fortunately, Roman, unaware of the battle of wills arcing between his uncle and myself, chose that moment to hop down from the adjoining bakery door and tug on my sleeve.

"Miss Tamsin, can I have my cookie now?"

Kat interrupted before I could answer. "Come with me, sport. We'll go get it." She held out a hand to him while reaching around the top of the door's shelf and unlocking it. Roman didn't wait for a second invitation. Grabbing her hand, he all but dragged her into Blessed Bee.

Just as the door began to swing shut, he poked his head around the jamb. "Take care of Gunnar for me!"

And then I was left alone with Raiden. Taking a calming breath, I turned back toward him. My stomach somersaulted. Jerk though he may be, he was also incredibly virile and sexy. And annoyed.

"We need to talk," he said for the second time.

"No, we really don't." I crossed my arms, glared at the door right behind him, and willed it open. "Go away."

He smirked, and the door barked shut.

Grinding my molars, I opened it again.

Looking bored, Raiden closed it.

I gave him a mental nudge, just enough to push him backward a step, then popped the door open. The bored expression was replaced by frustration when he got popped in the ass. He stalked toward me, slamming the portal hard enough to rattle the glass that time.

When we were nearly toe to toe, he said, "Stop that." Like I was a kid, being reprimanded by a parent.

I shrugged. "Get over yourself. It's my store and

my door." It swung wide, inviting a blistering gust of wind in with it. "And FYI, I could do this all day."

"And I could do it for centuries." He leaned down until our lips nearly touched. "But I think you already know that."

Centuries, my ass. The guy wasn't much older than me. And who knew what other delusions he harbored?

Regardless, his midnight-blue eyes shimmered with sensual promise, shooting arrows of desire straight to my core. *Goddess.* Rowena had been right. It *was* hot in there. I shifted away, though I had to fight my traitorous body to obey.

"Oh, right...the whole demigod, immortal rumor. How could I forget?"

"Rumor...." He straightened with a confused expression. As if nobody had ever doubted his purported genetics before?

For some reason, a flash of doubt and regret niggled at me. He obviously believed he was the son of a god. And I'd never liked making anyone feel badly about where they came from, even if it might be all in their head. For goddess's sake, witches had been defending their beliefs and heritage for centuries, and still were. Nevertheless, while Raiden had some pretty amazing abilities, he was nothing more than a *very* powerful witch.

Not a demigod.

Since they don't exist.

Chapter Six

Raiden blew out a breath. "Can we talk?"

My earlier conversation with Kat filtered through my mind. Ignorance is bliss, and I wasn't interested in hearing what he had to say. Because once I allowed that, my life would never be the same.

"I can't just leave. I'm working, in case you haven't noticed."

With an almost imperceptible droop of his shoulders, he uttered the one word I never expected: "Please."

Considering, I stared out the front window. Main Street teamed with shoppers, and runners, and dog-walkers, many of whom would be stopping into one or both of the bakeries. I couldn't leave Kat to manage both on the busiest day of the week.

Beginning to refuse, I met his compelling gaze. More desire stirred in my belly, and the crystals sang in my bosom. Right then, I was totally ready for them to work their magic and make me discerning and enlightened, as long as I could do that with Raiden, even if he was annoying.

Kat was *so* on her own.

"Let me get a sweater."

Moments later, we walked silently toward the gazebo in the center of the village, with the porky Gunnar toddling ahead of us, sniffing every bush, pole, and hydrant along the way. I waved to a couple of workers who'd just finishing hanging colorful banners in preparation for the upcoming Samhain celebration, my favorite holiday.

Wet wind blustered around us, even though the sun shone. Not a strand of Raiden's glossy black hair moved, while mine whipped around in an ever-tangling red curly cloud, finally coming loose from its ponytail holder. Raiden bent to retrieve the elastic band and handed it to me.

"Can you please turn off the weather?" I asked. After securing my hair again, I hunched into the oversized cable-knit sweater I'd grabbed from the hatch of my car. I gave one of the sleeves a surreptitious sniff, praying the lamb's wool didn't smell like eau de Merlin.

Raiden guided me up the steps of the gazebo and gestured toward a bench before scooping up Gunnar, who struggled with the steep climb. I thought Raiden had ignored my request, but as soon as we sat, the wind died down to a whisper and, even in the shade, I felt remarkably warmer.

He shifted to face me, his face going all demanding again. "Let's get a couple of things clear—"

I held up a palm. "Hold it right there. You may think you're a demigod, which you aren't, because they don't exist, but the last thing I'm going to do is follow your commandments. Or dictates. Or whatever it is fake demigods like to do."

He raised an *are-you-done* eyebrow then said, "Allow me to rephrase...I'm sorry if I made you uncomfortable last night."

Uncomfortable? Not the word I would have used to describe how he'd made me feel the night before. Then again, I wasn't about to stroke his inflated ego either. One little apology did not make up for all of the other things he'd done and said to me in the short time since he'd landed in my life.

"I can handle uncomfortable. What I won't accept is being insulted, or criticized, or made to feel unworthy of some misplaced sense of destiny, by an arrogant dickhead with a deity complex."

There. I'd done it. Completely thrown *do no harm* out the window by accusing him of doing what I'd just done—criticized and insulted.

Raiden stared at me for so long, I resisted the urge to squirm. A cold, damp breeze rolled across the wooden floorboards and slithered up my body. Oh, great. I'd angered him.

Again.

He set the dog on the plank floor and Gunnar immediately rolled on his back, no doubt looking for a belly rub. Raiden gave him a few scratches then looked up at me.

"We do exist."

My sigh left little doubt what a crock I thought that was. "I don't know what sort of bedtime stories your mom told you, but that's all they were—fairy tales." I watched his long, tanned fingers stroke the pup's pink, freckled tummy. My own tummy itched with jealousy. If Gunnar's lolling tongue was any indication, the strokes were sheer ecstasy. I stifled a shiver, and not from the chill in the air. Raiden rose and pulled his hand out of the loop handle of the leash then all but shoved it into my hand.

In a weird, unexplainable moment of panic, I asked, "Where are you going?"

"If I had a choice, anywhere but here, believe me."

What was *that* supposed to mean? I wasn't the weirdo here.

He began to pace then halted with his back to me and gripped one of the posts. "Do you have any idea what I'm going through?"

Uh...no? Other than you're crazy as a bedbug?

A really hot bedbug.

"I think you're delusional, but something tells me you've been that way for quite a while," I offered helpfully. Why was I baiting him? Other than being an overbearing and arrogant dickhead, he really didn't deserve it. What he deserved was my pity, the poor guy.

Thunder cracked and a bolt of lightning hit a manhole cover in the middle of Main Street directly across from us, sending it skidding a good half block down the asphalt. Gunnar yelped and leapt into my lap, no small feat for his porky self, while shouts of alarm echoed from pedestrians as they scattered away from the smoking wound in the road.

Holy crap on a cracker!

Shoving off the bench, I cuddled the trembling dog in my arms and stalked toward Raiden. "Quit playing evil weatherman, you fool! It doesn't impress me, and that was just a tad dangerous, don't you think?"

Anger and maybe some frustration flowed off him in waves. "I don't have to impress you. I only have to convince you, princess."

He did not just call me that.

"I don't know what kind of game you're playing, and why you think I'd play it with you, but I'm not interested."

Biting cold wind gusted through the gazebo again and Gunnar shook harder. Without a word, Raiden unbuttoned his coat, plucked Gunnar from my arms and wrapped him inside it for warmth. The selfless action chipped at my hardened resolve not to trust the man.

Fatigue etched his face, although the arrogance hadn't faded. "So that's it then."

Get while the gettin's good, Tamsin. "That's it. Find another clueless witch to buy your loser demigod story." Untangling the leash from my wrist, I dropped it. "But I have to tell you, it was one hell of a brilliant pick-up line."

Stalking back to The Blessed Bee, I had the uncomfortable sensation of his eyes boring into my back.

Back at the shop, Roman sat on the counter by the register, swinging his legs and licking green frosting off his fingers. "Hey, Miss Tamsin! These cookies are awesome. Have you tried them?"

Leave it to him to lighten my mood. "Why yes,

Roman, I have."

He slurped milk from a to-go cup and grinned. "Uncle Raiden is going to love them, too. Miss Kat let me decorate one for him."

And leave it to the mere mention of his uncle's name to darken my mood again. I only nodded to avoid snarling. Kat stood nearby, counted receipts and grinned.

Roman set the cup aside and jumped down. "Where's Gunnar?"

"Your uncle has him in the park across the street. He'll be here soon." I glanced over at Kat with a pleading look.

"Roman, why don't you go decorate a couple more cookies?" Kat pointed toward the kitchen. "I left them on counter for you."

Once he'd scooted out of the room, she said, "Was that loverboy who detonated the manhole cover?"

Ignoring the cutsie nickname, I snorted. "The very same."

She chuckled. "Roman said, 'uh oh, Miss Tamsin

just made Uncle Raiden mad again.'"

"That's not even funny." I went behind the counter and began to make some green tea. Kat, being the smarter of the two of us, remained silent.

After adding honey and lemon to my brew, I leaned against the counter and sipped. Unbidden images filled my mind of the erotic things I'd seen Raiden and I doing together, and the crystals against my breastbone warmed in response. A corresponding warmth flowed through my veins that I couldn't blame on the tea. The compulsion I felt toward the man warred with the survival instinct to run. He was sex, and danger, and something else, something indefinable. Actually, that wasn't quite true. I could define it if I chose to. *The One* being the probable definition. I squashed the notion like a bug and took another sip, rubbing my sternum as the stones grew warmer.

The bakery's front door swung wide and Raiden stood on the threshold, holding a damp, whining Gunnar. Rain pattered softly behind them.

Our eyes met, his dark and flat. And the light

played tricks on his handsome face because he appeared even more tired than he had when I'd left him a few short minutes earlier.

And his glorious black hair was wet.

Weather of any kind never touched him, at least not what I'd seen thus far, and revelation that he was suddenly not so immune to it startled me, but worse, alarmed me, and I refused to contemplate why. The crystals burned then, not enough to harm me, but sending a big, fat *beware* message.

"Do you mind sending Roman out?" Raiden's voice was quiet, almost weak-sounding. "I don't want to come in here with the dog."

As though he had puppy radar, Roman ran out of the kitchen, heading for Gunnar. Wiggling like a piglet, the dog yipped until Raiden set him on the sidewalk.

While Roman crouched beside him to let Gunnar lick frosting off his hands, Raiden said, "Good-bye, Tamsin," and shut the door behind them.

"Well, that sounded final," Kat murmured.

"Shut up," I said around a baseball-sized lump in

my throat.

***

By 2:00 a.m. that night I'd given up hope of falling asleep. My mind whirled with thoughts of Raiden and, no matter how hard I tried, I couldn't get that last image of him standing in the doorway of Blessed Bee, looking drained and dripping wet, out of my mind or rid myself of the swirling emotions he evoked.

I worked on lesson plans, tried to read a chapter from a musty old volume of *The History of Spells* I'd picked up at Flysmacker's Booke Shop next door to the bakery, but my brain refused to focus on anything for more than ten seconds. Finally giving up, I wandered downstairs to light a fire and get a cup of mint tea, thinking maybe warmth inside and out would make me sleepy. The air had turned frosty enough I had to pull on a pair of ancient pink-flannel Hello Kitty pajamas I'd had since college. The cheerful name still blazoned across the top, but most of the K in Kitty had worn away a bit and looked more like a T.

Hello Titty.

Fortunately, nobody ever saw the jammies but me.

After discovering I'd used the last match from the box on the mantle, I dug in the junk drawer in the kitchen for a lighter without luck. No surprise. The entire day had been one disappointment after another. Setting the kettle on to boil, I stood in front of the sink and stared out the window at my tiny backyard. Leaves skittered under the lone tree and frost sparkled like diamonds on the grass and porch. Samhain would be a chilly affair this year. I'd have to ask Kat to pick up more cider from the orchard near her house. Hot cider and doughnuts were always a hit during the festival.

Oh hell, who cared about frost, cider, or festivals? I couldn't have cared less because of the one thing that hovered like a nagging old witch in my subconscious. Why fight it? My libido refused to be denied, and my thoughts drifted to Raiden again, damn the man. For a delusional un-demigod, he certainly liked to poke into my head a lot. I wrapped my arms around my waist and groaned in frustration.

Just as I plopped the tea ball into the cup and poured water over it, I heard scuffling out front and then a knock. Thinking I had to be hearing things, I glanced at the clock on the stove—2:30 a.m. From the sink, I can see clear through the house to the front door, and I froze while I stared at it, the hair on my nape and arms standing at attention. My senses knew who'd come a-calling...had been waiting for him, in fact....

Raiden.

Without hesitating, and against all common sense, I walked on shaky legs and opened the door. *Wow.* Right then, I could almost believe he was the son of a god. Big and beautiful in an utterly masculine way, the guy was total model material. His skin and lips were flushed from the cold and the wind had tousled his long, inky hair the way my fingers wanted to do. And dressed in black, from the peacoat to jeans and leather boots, he took my breath away.

Could have been the wind gusting in behind him, but I went with the former explanation.

My heart skipped a beat then stopped when I focused on his eyes. The dark shadows present earlier had deepened to a bruise-blue, and deep lines etched the corners. Without thinking, and being the nurturer that made me rescue stray animals and the occasional middle-of-the-night delusional man, I reached for his hand and pulled him in. After closing out the harsh weather, I stared at him. In the overhead light, his appearance frightened me even more. He didn't move, only stood silently.

I let go of his hand. "Are you sick?"

"Hardly." The denial rang clear, but the voice wasn't the hard, strong one I could have picked out of a crowd. The weak tone was almost as scary as his appearance.

I frowned. "What are you doing here?" Even though for some odd reason, it made perfect sense to have a man I barely knew show up on my doorstep in the dead of night. No doubt about it, shit had been weird since he'd walked into my life. Why should this surprise me?

Ignoring my question, he unbuttoned the coat and shrugged out of it.

Since it appeared he planned to settle in for a while, I said, "Um...have a seat. Do you want something to drink?"

"Whatever you're having."

After getting his tea prepared, I turned from the stove and jerked back with a yelp of surprise. Raiden hadn't taken a seat. Instead, he leaned against the counter nearby, watching me.

"Careful." He smirked, taking the mug and setting it back on the granite.

I swallowed hard. His body heat penetrated the cool air between us, and when he moved closer, warning tingles of electricity arced between us. *Not this again.* After insomnia the night before, a really long, strange day, and what looked to be another sleepless night, I couldn't take even the most lackluster of orgasms. Really.

He traced a fingertip up my pink fleece top, grazed over a traitorously straining nipple and rested his palm over Hello Titty. "Nice," he said.

My face burned. *Good-bye Titty. You, my dear jammies, are headed for the rag bag.* I slapped his hand away. "If I'd known you were coming, I would have worn something sexier."

Oh goddess, I didn't just say that.

Lifting the hand again, he teased one nipple with the pad of his thumb and the corner of his mouth twitched. "I never said I didn't like what you're wearing." He tipped my chin up with his free hand and bent until his lips hovered over mine. I tensed and closed my eyes, ready to be blown away by his gorgeous mouth. It never happened. He pulled back and said, "But I did come here to talk."

Not again. He'd obviously forgotten the last time we'd talked hadn't gone so well.

He grabbed both cups of tea and sauntered toward the living room then settled on the couch. I huffed behind him, following like an obedient puppy. When I went to sit in a chair opposite him, he shook his head. "By me."

I scowled, but continued the puppy routine,

although I did give another huff of anger to let him know I didn't appreciate his highhandedness. Then a thought struck me. "Where's Roman?" Goddess, Raiden hadn't left the boy alone, had he?

Raiden cleared his throat. "He's with Katarina."

My scowl deepened. "Why?"

He took a sip of his tea. Grimacing, he set the mug down again. "She showed up and told me to get my ass over here and play the god card with you." At my dumbstruck expression, he added, "Her words, not mine."

How dare she? "That's it. I'm going to fire her."

He smiled. "She's your business partner."

"I'll find a way."

This wasn't any of Kat's concern and why did she keep trying to convince me to give Raiden a chance? Her showing up at his house in the middle of the night to play matchmaker-slash-babysitter?

So fired.

He watched me wordlessly until the room echoed with loud silence. Finally, I said, "So...talk."

Scraping a palm over the black stubble on his

jaw, he continued to stare at me then stood abruptly. "It's freezing in here."

I rose as well. "I was going to light a fire, but couldn't find any match—" The logs in the fireplace roared to life as though a blowtorch had detonated under them. "Okay then."

Raiden warmed his hands. "And here I thought you were a witch."

I narrowed my eyes at his continual arrogance. Evidently, he'd forgotten the head-busting flyboy trip he'd taken mere hours earlier in my classroom. "I'm a spellcaster and precog. I can't just make things burst into flame. Not without forethought, anyway." This obviously not being one of those times.

And then I was being crowded by a large, solid body. Teetering, I gasped and groped for the couch to break my fall then got jerked upright again by an iron grip around my waist. Our bodies were locked tight, groin and thighs getting very personal. Oh, sweet goddess, he was hard. *Everywhere.*

"I can make lots of things burst into flame," he murmured.

70

A kiss can be described with words like clinical, sensual, even delicious. But when Raiden lowered his mouth on mine...there were no words. So, I moaned instead. Forget the *demi*: at that moment the man was, without a doubt, an unadulterated god. His forearm dug into the small of my back, lifting me up until only my toes remained on the floor, and a prominent erection rubbed against my core, way distracting. Oh, the promise of it. I moaned again and wound my arms around his neck to keep him right where he was. After an altogether too-short joining, he unwrapped himself from my hold and pulled back.

Let down, I hid my disappointment by saying in as unaffected a voice as I could manage, "Unless you have a really good reason for being here, I don't want this."

He smirked and grazed his thumbs across Hello Titty, finding the sensitive nipples underneath. The guy was definitely a boob man. "Liar."

I slapped his hands down for the second time. "Stop it." My anger rose with humiliation—an understandable emotion. But when unexplainable tears pricked and then threatened to well, I turned away. My clit pulsed in time with my hammering heart. How unfair that I had to be so attracted to a man—a plain old witch—who had illusions of grandeur. I mean, any witch with developed powers can cast a sex spell, weave a little nookie magic, and....

Wait a second. I ran a finger over my lower lip and frowned. *Any witch with developed powers can cast a sex spell.* And keep it going for as long as he wanted.

Unless there was some reason for those powers to be taken away, Raiden, should have no problem continuing to bewitch me, turn me on, give me monumental orgasms. Instead, his abilities appeared to have declined. Sure, I was very turned on right then. But that was the extent of it. The night before, he'd given me a heady release with barely a touch of his lips. But the lip-lock we'd just shared had been mere delightful foreplay.

So...unless part of his diabolical plan for seducing me included convincing me my disbelief in his godly genetics somehow weakened him, which was ludicrous since the guy obviously loved to lord his strength over me, and what was the point in convincing me of that anyway, then....

Quelling rising, unexplainable panic, I turned around again, met his eyes...and stared into his soul. "Let's talk."

Chapter Seven

Raiden all but fell onto the couch, as if his legs were rubber. I'd like to think I was the reason for that, but his ashen skin and the circles under his eyes told another story. The man was seriously fatigued. Well, it *had* been one heck of a long day that seemed to have no end. But I doubted sleep deprivation was the real cause.

He leaned forward and rested his elbows on his knees. Hanging his head, he blew out a breath. Then said in a low, tired voice, "I never thought this would be so difficult."

I frowned. "What's so difficult?"

"Finding you."

Nonplussed, I didn't know how to respond to that. Difficult? He hadn't exactly paved the road to mated bliss with his arrogance. And yes, I wanted to accept that we were supposed to be together. I'd taken a gander at his thoughts, and any decent precog knows when images like his are wishful thinking and

74

when they're future events waiting to unfold. And it isn't uncommon for witches to know within moments when they'd found their soul mate. Our view of the world is different than humankind's and that view has served us well, especially in love.

But I wasn't comfortable settling down with him. The *difficulty* Raiden and I were having was all about his claim of mythical godliness and that annoying arrogance he attached to it. It frightened me he believed he was the son of a god. As attractive and intelligent as Raiden might be, that belief was the deal-breaker.

Unfortunately, the future can be changed, regardless of what I'd seen in his head. Those events weren't written in stone. We all control our own destinies. And even though he and I had just met, it hurt my heart to know we'd have to part ways, no matter how aggravated he'd made me, and in such a short period of time. His words when we met still stung. Regardless what he felt about me, being a schoolteacher *and* a businesswoman is damned respectable. If not exhausting.

Putting my defenses up , I said, "Yes, you made it clear I wasn't what you expected. Your disappointment was pretty obvious."

He lifted his head, some of the old Raiden arrogance back in his eyes. "Then let me make this clear; I *never* said I was disappointed." The words thrilled and saddened me.

We both looked away then and stared at the fire crackling merrily.

"Look, Tamsin...I don't have the energy to argue." He raked a hand through his hair.

Argue. Ha, that's all we'd done since we met. And without the benefit of make-up sex afterward. I shrugged away that thought before it took root.

"Then why are you here?" I asked. "It's the middle of the night, and I have to be at the shop in a couple of hours."

"I wanted to try one more time to convince you I am what I say I am." He sounded almost defeated, his voice low and barely audible.

Damn it. Why did he keep pushing? "Raiden, it's obvious we have great chemistry. You don't have to pretend to be something you aren't."

The guard in front of the fireplace whooshed past my head, through the living room, and slid across the kitchen floor. It spun wildly for a few seconds before coming to a halt near the fridge with a dull clang. A black skid mark marred the tile.

Thank the goddess there were no manhole covers in my house. It probably would've decapitated me. "Really?" I asked while hoping the hot metal hadn't destroyed anything out there. I was still making payments on that fridge. "Are we having another tantrum?"

"Sorry. Gods tend to get pissed when they're called liars."

I suddenly felt as exhausted as he looked. After a few moments, I said, "Okay. Look. It's late and I'm going to turn into the Wicked Witch of the West if I don't get at least a couple hours of sleep." I held up a hand before he could refute the claim I wasn't already said witch. "Just tell me why I should believe you're a god and we can both get some rest."

His gaze rested on the fireplace, as though he

were looking into the flames for guidance. Finally, he said, "My mother warned me it would be this way. I didn't believe her."

I don't care what Kat had told me; this guy was definitely leaning toward mama's-boy zone. "You seem to put an awful lot of stock in what your mother thinks."

Raiden turned toward me, eyes narrowed. "I have no reason not to. She's *Moerae*."

I reared back as though he'd struck me. "That's impossible," I whispered. Feeling faint, I rose slowly and backed away a few steps until the heat from the fire threatened to singe my ratty pajama pants. I crossed my arms over Hello Titty. "I'm not a fool, Raiden."

Sweet goddess. I truly didn't know whether to laugh or cry. He'd nearly had me believing he was the son of a god. I *wanted* to believe it. But the son of a god and a *Moerae*?

We witches all have a healthy belief in fate. We're born with it and have a destiny, life being a journey and all that. The choices we make determine how our destinies play out and can take many twists and turns. *Like this one.*

The one thing we can't predict is the outcome of those twists and turns. We can guess, we can hope for the best, and goddess knew enough of us prayed to her and other deities on a regular basis for an outcome we can live with. But ultimately, we all go through life blind, our decisions are ours, let the chips fall where they may.

The *Moerae* bypass that pesky rule. They know what's going to happen to us and have no issue with taking that knowledge and manipulating it. For better or worse.

Plus, a true *Moerae* is exceedingly rare. Like, one-born-per-millennium rare. And the idea of having having a *Moerae* mother-in-law? Wouldn't *that* add unwanted spice to my life.

Close to tears, I asked. "Why are you doing this?"

He eased up to his feet. I swear I heard a stifled groan, the kind an old man would make. I refused to feel guilty about any role I may have played in that elder-moment. He'd just thrown me the biggest curveball in...well, hours.

"I wasn't going to tell you. At least not for a while." His near-black gaze met mine and wouldn't let go.

Unable to back away without getting burned, I hugged myself tighter. "What...you didn't think I'd want to know the man declaring he's my future demigod mate is also the son of a witch who can change *destinies*?" The last word ended in a shriek. Horrified at that and just about everything frankly, I burst into tears and spun away.

Damn the man! He'd almost—*almost*—had me.

Firm hands gripped my shoulders and tried to turn me back around, but I wouldn't budge. I'm the world's ugliest crier—red nose, puffy eyes, blotchy face. No matter how much I despised him at that moment, I didn't want him to see me like that.

A calm voice, level with my ear, said in the sincerest tone, "I'm sorry, love."

Hunching into myself, I let the tears roll. How could life be so unfair? Less than forty-eight hours earlier, I'd been a content, if exhausted, preschool teacher-slash-bakery owner. My house (and my refrigerator) was nearly paid for, I had a sweet ride in the driveway, even went on the occasional date with guys my dad *would* approve of. And now...that life seemed both distant and utterly boring. Even though my only remaining option was to kick Raiden to the curb and return to my old life, both of which would just about kill me, I knew what I had to do.

On a shuddery breath, I swiped my arm across my face and faced him. His sympathetic expression, one I'm pretty sure had to be rarer than a blood moon during Samhain, changed to resignation when I said, "I can't do this. Please go."

Ten minutes later, I settled under the covers in my chilly bedroom with a steamy cup of peppermint tea and rested my head back against the headboard. *What just happened?* Raiden left without another word, simply picked up his coat and poof—gone. More than in the literal sense, too. I saw the look on his face...he wasn't coming back.

Lifting *The History of Spells* tome off my nightstand, I opened it to a random page. The leather spine cracked in protest. The book had to be a hundred years old, if not more. The font was old, too, sort of manuscripty-looking in many places, a bit hard to read. I ran my fingers over the yellowed page, loving the musty, dusty scent of the paper, thrilled once more I'd found the book at Flysmackers.

Pausing mid-stroke, I frowned. *What the....* The word jumped out like a lightning strike. *Moerae.* I quickly scanned a few pages before and after the one with the offending word, but that particular page seemed to be the only one referring to the *Moerae.* What were the chances I'd turn to that particular page tonight of all nights? With shaking hands clutching the old text, I began to read. All about the role *Moerae* played in each of our lives. Every single day.

An hour later, lightheaded and queasy, and not from lack of shuteye, I set *The History of Spells* back on the nightstand. All I really wanted to do was turn off the light, bury my head under the pillow, and cry myself to sleep. Instead, I headed for the shower, intent on going to work and forgetting all about a certain demigod and his *Moerae* mother.

After toweling off, I started to throw Hello Titty in the hamper but stuffed the pajamas in the bathroom trash can instead. The last thing I needed were reminders or memories of Raiden. Pretty sure I had enough of those to last a lifetime, thank you.

With a heavy heart, I headed toward the armoire, thinking a pair of jeans and comforting cable-knit sweater Katarina had made me seemed like a solid wardrobe choice. Something crinkled under my bare foot, and I glanced down. A creamy-white piece of parchment-like paper lay on the carpet. Picking it up, I caught a whiff of musty-dusty. The thing must have fallen out of *The History of Spells*. Somebody's leftover bookmark, probably. Flipping the paper over, I jolted at the words written on it in precise block letters, almost like a printer had made them.

I am your destiny.

Driving to The Blessed Bee in total darkness was nothing new for me. But driving in a mental fog and bawling like a baby was. I arrived in the small parking lot behind the shop at the same time Kat pulled in. She appeared to be struggling with something in the back seat, so I dried my eyes and went over to help her.

Roman jumped out just as I got around to the driver's side.

"Hey, Miss Tamsin! Kat brought me to work because Uncle Raiden is packing." With a very adult gesture, he waved away any worries I may have about his being there. "I'm here to help you in the bakery. Just tell me what to do."

I cast a questioning glance at Katarina, who raised an eyebrow at my splotchy face. *We need to talk*, she mouthed.

We sure as hell did *need to talk*. Not about Roman, but about other, just-as-important stuff. He marched ahead of us to unlock the back door with the key Kat had handed him. After working at it for a few moments, he gave it back to her. "I think the lock's broken."

Kat smiled. "It's tricky, for sure." She pretended

to struggle with it for a couple of seconds then pushed. "Open sesame."

Roman giggled, jumped up the step, and headed straight through the kitchen and out to the bakery. As the door swung shut behind him, he called, "Do you have any of those cookies with the brown and white frosting left?"

I started to suggest he have a healthy whole-grain, nut, and dried fruit-infested breakfast cookie, but Kat cut me off. "Sure! You can have one." She followed him, and I heard her muffled, "And a glass of milk."

A minute later she came back into the kitchen and leaned a hip against the stainless steel island that separated us. "I started the coffees. Should be ready in a few."

"Good. Thanks." I lifted my chin to gesture toward the bakery. "What's he doing here?" Not that I minded, but when Kat and I got into the finer details of the night before, including her sending Raiden to my house in the wee hours, I didn't feel like having the little boy see me cry. Because it was inevitable that I would in all my red-eyed, blotchy-faced glory.

"Like he told you...his uncle is packing to leave. Evidently, Roman's mother and father are coming home this afternoon." She yawned so hard, her jaw should've cracked. "And I'm really tired. That kid is an insomniac. Do you know how many games of Chutes & Ladders we played?"

Like I cared, but I shook my head no.

"Goddess help me, I suffered through twelve of them. And the only reason I agreed to that was because I had to dissuade him from playing Cards Against Humanity." Kat rolled her eyes.

I barely caught that last line, and clueless what the card game was, I murmured, "Isn't there a kids' version?"

She gaped. "Um, no. That would be a really, really bad thing."

Okay, I'd take her word for it.

"So....." She scraped a metal stool over to the table and sat, grabbing a day-old carrot flaxseed muffin for her efforts. Tearing a chunk off the top, she said, "Tell me what's going on."

86

I copied her, swung a stool over and snagged a muffin. "Well, as you know"—I took a bite of the muffin—"Raiden dropped by last night. Correction—this morning."

"Uh huh."

"Kat, you didn't have any right to do—"

"Oh, whatever! It was for your own good. We can hash that out later." She waved her hand, tossing crumbs across the steel surface. "Get on with the story."

The bit of muffin I'd managed to swallow turned to sawdust in my throat and all of a sudden, I wasn't so sure I could even discuss Raiden. And oh goddess! He was leaving? Sure, I'd sent him away, but...leaving!

I cleared my throat. "He looked awful when he got to my house. I think he's sick." Talk about a stall tactic. Under-the-weather Raiden was the least of my worries.

"Tamsin, he *is* sick."

My heart thumped and I froze. "What?"

Kat threw a hunk of muffin at me in disgust.

"Damn, girl! Are you that blind?"

Bewildered, I could only shake my head. What was I missing? It seemed like everything I said, she was one step ahead of me.

She gave me an exaggerated huff of annoyance. "We studied the history of the gods in school. Don't you remember that?"

"That was seventh grade. What girl remembers anything that happened in seventh grade except maybe starting her period and getting a training bra?"

"Here's a refresher," said the former middle school valedictorian, ignoring me. "In *The Lives of the Gods*, we learned that while gods are immortal, including offspring who may be of a dual nature, they're inherently super-beings, with all the strengths and powers necessary to fulfill their godly obligations. But they have one major Achilles' heel."

I shrugged. "Ohhhh-kay."

"Wow, you really weren't paying attention back then."

I held up two fingers. "Period. Training bra. Moving on."

"A god's Achilles' heel is his mate. Once he finds her, or vice-versa as the case may be, he is able to gain even more power and strength from the union. If she rejects or betrays him, he weakens. The stronger a mate's hold on the god, the weaker he will become if she doesn't return his affections. "

"Hold that thought." I ran out to the bakery floor, checked on Roman, who was watching a video on our handheld iPad cash-register thingy, grabbed two coffees—hazelnut for Kate, dark roast for me—and scooted back to the kitchen.

Kat pulled a carton of half-and-half out of the walk-in cooler and poured a healthy shot into her cup. She pushed the creamer over to me, along with a packet of sugar.

After we'd finished doctoring our brews, she said, "So, that's why Raiden is sick."

I blew on my hot liquid and frowned. "He's sick because he has an Achilles' heel?" I hadn't noticed him limping or anything.

"*You* are his Achilles' heel, you dope." When I didn't respond to what she obviously thought was an earth-shattering revelation, she added, "*You* are making him sick, Tam."

Slowly setting the cup on the table, I frowned then gave her a small laugh. "We barely know each other." Then, thinking about that, I dropped my gaze from her own knowing one. Hadn't I admitted to myself the previous night, er, morning, he was my mate? Something she'd clearly figured out already.

I mumbled, "Besides, how can I be responsible for his state of health when I don't even believe in that demigod business?"

The air between us bristled with tension. I snuck a peek at her. Her eyes were narrowed.

"Do not make me throw this last morsel of organic goodness at your head, Tam. Because you know I will."

I raised my palms in defeat. "Fine. Fine! I give. I'm a believer, okay?"

The hunk of organic goodness was laid to rest next to her coffee. "And?"

"What...there's more? What do you want from me?"

The swinging door behind her opened and Roman strode in. "Spongebob is over and I'm still hungry. Can I have another cookie?"

"No," we replied in unison.

I snapped a banana off a pile lying nearby and handed him one. "Here. I'm pretty sure you know how to work that iPad better than either of us do. Go find another video to watch. A long one."

He bobbed his head and darted back out with the fruit. "Okay!"

"Hey, keep it PG though! I don't want any calls from your mother," I called after him.

Kat snickered. "You are going to make such a lousy parent."

"Tell me about it." I took a sip of my now-lukewarm coffee.

We sat in silence for a few moments. The elephant in the room took a seat nearby. We pretended he wasn't there. The sappy theme from some kids' movie filtered in from the other room.

Finally, Kat said, "You know I know everything that's going on, right?"

I planted my elbows on the table, rested my chin in one palm, and stared over at her. "Not everything." *I hope.*

"Let me spell it out for you. I'm a precog, just like you. Maybe not as good as you are, but for some odd reason, I've seen enough that's going on to know...well, let's put it this way, I've seen more than I care to know." She squinted at the ceiling as though recalling. "Way more."

My face burned. *Please goddess, not everything!*

She yawned and looked back down at me. "Yeah, so now I'm just wondering when you're going to figure out the demigod of your dreams is walking out of your life because you're too stubborn to admit the truth?"

Damn them to hell and back, but the waterworks started rolling again. "I know what he is, Kat. I believe he's a demigod." Holy hell, those were words I never thought I'd utter. But in for a penny, in for a pound. "There's one other thing though. Something huge. And I can't live with it."

"Hmmm." She tapped her chin with her index

finger. "Could it be *Moerae*?"

If I weren't holding my mouth closed with one hand, it would've dropped. "Crap on a cracker, you *do* see everything!"

She waved that off as though it were a compliment rather than an accusation. "Raiden's mother is a *Moerae*. And that's a problem because?"

I straightened, anger finding the shut-off valve on my waterworks. "Would you want a mother-in-law who could manipulate your life? Your mate's life? Your *children's* lives? Because that's what *Moerae* do. They can twist destinies if it suits them. I don't want that."

"I'll give you another *Lives of the Gods* refresher...this latest factoid suddenly makes the whole annoying demigod problem seem pretty trivial, doesn't it?"

I sneered but refrained from a comeback. A big pet peeve of mine is *I-told-you-so*.

Kat said, "The *Moerae* have a code of ethics and morals. Most don't abuse the incredible privilege they have. Some are bad eggs, just like some people are in any position of power."

"She spawned Raiden. How good can she really be if she let that happen to herself?" I griped.

"Yeah, gee, super-hot, sexy guy who happens to be so head-over-heels in lust with you—which is a great start to a lasting relationship in my opinion—that he's made himself sick over you." She blew out a breath. "Seriously, just take that man out back and shoot him."

Har dee har har. I narrowed my eyes at her, but didn't say anything. She had me thinking, but not sold.

"I guess then, the real question is this: do you want Raiden badly enough to let Mama Alexsander *maybe possibly* fiddle with your future, or are you going to take a pass and let that man get away?"

Roman took that moment to barrel through the swinging door. "Hey, Uncle Raiden is here and he wants to see you, Miss Tams—" He skidded to a halt. "Why are you crying?"

Was I crying again? *Oh, hell.* "I was chopping onions," I lied.

He stood on tiptoes and peered over the edge of the high table. "I don't see any onions."

Kat lifted him off the ground and swung him over her shoulder. "She was only thinking about chopping onions. That always makes her weepy." Her gaze found mine. "She's real sensitive that way." Setting Roman on the edge of the table, she covered his ears with her palms, tipped her head toward the bakery floor, and hissed, "Get your butt out there and cut that poor man a break before he dies all over the place."

By the time I worked up the nerve to go out and see Raiden, I was in near heart failure. The only thing keeping it ticking was probably my knees knocking together. I found Raiden standing inside near the front window, his back to me.

Roman'd obviously had no problem working the lock on the front door to let Raiden in, but it concerned me the security alarm hadn't started squealing.

Raiden eyed me over his shoulder and must have caught my glance at the nearby security panel. "I turned off the alarm." He snapped his fingers. *Easy as starting a blaze in your fireplace*, they seemed to say.

"It's supposed to be spell-proof." I murmured, coming around the counter cautiously.

He sighed, but his voice was calm when he said, "Not everything I can do involves witchcraft, or haven't you figured that out yet?"

Our eyes met, his the dark midnight-blue that made my heart ache knowing every time I looked into his nephew's gaze, it would make me think of Raiden. I checked him over and wanted to weep at how beautiful, if tired, he looked, dressed all in black like he had been when we'd met eons ago at Meet-the-Teacher Night. His drawn face, etched with what I now knew was caused by an Achilles' heel, namely me, caused massive guilt to fill me, making the weeping even harder to keep under control.

I was a total mess.

He approached and stopped a couple of feet away. "I came to say good-bye. I wasn't going to, but I just...." Swiping a hand over his face, he said, "Hell, I don't know why I thought this was a good idea. You let me know how you wanted things to go last night."

I'd been a stupid, clueless fool a few hours earlier. If there's a self-flagellation spell, point me in that direction. Why had everyone else seen what was right in front of me, but me? And yet, at that moment, I froze. My tongue stuck to the roof of my mouth, and I couldn't confirm or deny what he so obviously asked: *Do you really want me to go?*

When I didn't say anything, he took that as his answer. Lifting a hand, he stroked my cheek.

"Be well, Tamsin."

And once again, in the space of a few hours, I watched him leave. This time really for good.

My feet felt glued to the tile and heavy as lead. My head ached from lack of sleep, dark roast über-caffeinated coffee, and grief. In a word: love-sick.

Raiden stepped off the curb and was halfway across the street before I found the strength to yank my feet out of the quicksand and move.

Racing out of the shop, I screamed his name and launched off the sidewalk. He spun toward me, his expression a mixture of surprise and joy that quickly turned to horror.

He raised his hands as if to stop me. "Tamsin! Stop!"

Oh hell, no. I'd stop when I was in his arms and not a second before.

The squeal of brakes registered and time slowed, but not in the good, Raiden's-controlling-the-space-time-continuum-again kind of way. I barely saw the front end of the minivan before I sailed through the air in the most bizarre, painless way. Sideways at first. Then backward.

Then nothing.

The burning agony started before I'd even opened my eyes. Fighting the pull of consciousness, I willed myself back to the darkness, but an insistent voice filled my head, the sound odd, as though filtered through a vacuum.

Tamsin. Stay with me.

In and out I traveled, until true consciousness won and I opened my eyes. Midnight-blue stared back. Raw relief etched Raiden's grim face.

"Don't move, love."

Naturally, the first thing I did was ignore him. If I could have, I would've yelped in pain, but could only manage a soft groan.

"Where do you hurt?" he asked.

"Everywhere," I whispered. I couldn't take my eyes off of him, finding strength in having him there. "Hurts to breathe."

"I'll bet."

Gasps and concerned murmurs floated around me, but I laid on the cold asphalt between two parked cars and couldn't see anyone. Katarina was somewhere nearby asking questions, and I heard Roman sobbing. Raiden asked her to take his nephew back inside. Did I look that bad?

When sirens approached, Raiden asked one of the rubberneckers to guide it over then began to rise.

"Don't leave me." A tear rolled down my temple, followed by another one.

He knelt back down again. "I'm right here."

As the sirens grew louder, panic filled me. I had to talk to Raiden right then, not later. Needed to tell him what he desperately needed to hear. I lifted a hand and covered his, tried to squeeze, got more burn for my efforts, and just let it rest there.

"I have to tell you something."

"Later, love."

"No, now." I shifted my eyes toward the squalling ambulance. Time was running out. "Do that thing with time. Make everything slow down, just until I can say what I need to."

The corner of his mouth lifted with regret, and he shook his head. "I can't. I don't have the strength to do that right now."

Achilles' heel. *Well, hell.*

"I'm sorry, Raiden." More tears.

He pulled a handkerchief out of his rear pocket—who carries them anymore—and dabbed my skin. But he didn't say a word. He waited.

"I know who and what you are. I'm sorry I didn't believe you. That's what I was coming out to tell you." More tears, more dabbing.

He stared at me so long, I thought he didn't believe me. Then, he closed his eyes and inhaled, sucking in air like a drowning man. And again. When he opened them once more, they were clear and bright.

Lifting an arm, he waved his hand...and time crawled. The siren became an annoying, low buzz. The clouds overhead sat motionless in the sky. Even the chilly breeze stopped.

"Talk," he ordered.

Ah, my Raiden was back.

I swallowed and winced. "I'm sorry," I said again. "I'm just really, really sorry." It was all I could say. I wanted to sob, but it hurt too much. "You don't deserve this. And I don't deserve you." At that point, tears were filling my ear. How gross.

He tilted his head and a narrowed gaze pierced my soul. "I never want to hear that again. You're mine. I've waited too long for you to let you go, especially now."

Really? And why did the arrogant ownership in the words seem like a lullaby right then?

"I made you sick. Kat says I'm your Achilles' heel."

He chuckled. "I'll take you any way I can get you."

"You have me."

Bending down, he placed his lips lightly on mine. "Did you find my note?"

I frowned, as much as my sore face would let me. Note? What no— Oh, goddess. *That* note.

"How did you put that in the book without my knowing?" I croaked.

"I put it in there a hundred years ago when it was new. That was my book; I trained from it."

Holy crap on a cracker. My head must have taken a hard knock or two during that unscheduled flight across the minivan's grille.

"But how did you know I'd find it one day?"

"Now how do you think I knew?" he asked, wiping more tears on what was once a pristine-white linen hankie.

When I didn't answer, he bent over again and whispered, "*Moerae*."

Chapter Eight

"You really don't have to do this, you know."

Raiden lowered me to the red plaid blanket he'd spread on the ground. "I told you I'd take care of you, and I am."

"My arm is broken, not my legs."

"I'm not listening," he said.

Another blanket appeared, probably conjured, and he laid it over my outstretched legs.

"Be right back." He headed back to his car. A minute later, he returned with a lidded wicker basket and a pillow. He handed it to me.

"What's this for?"

"In case you want to lie down." He smirked. "And get comfortable."

Oh. I definitely want to lie down.

Crouching beside me, he opened the basket and pulled out a thermos of hot cider and bag of doughnuts, still slightly warm, both courtesy of Katarina. He poured the cider into two glasses and passed one to me.

"Blessed Samhain," we toasted together.

He rose and walked over to the huge pile of logs several feet away. Snapping his fingers, he set it on fire and stepped back when it roared to life. After settling down at my side, he asked, "Are you warm enough?"

"Not really." Before he could play nursemaid some more, I pulled the blanket on my legs over to cover his as well.

Grinning, he adjusted the pillow behind his head then wrapped an arm around me and pulled me down. I rested my head on his chest and tucked my bad arm to my side. It complained, but I didn't. The accident could have been far worse. Bruised ribs, broken wing, lots of cuts and scrapes, and one hot boyfriend later...worth every ache and pain.

"It feels strange celebrating Samhain out here."

Raiden angled his head to look down at me. "Why?"

"For as long as I can remember, I've spent it at the park in town with everyone. It's one of the reasons I wanted to buy the bakery when it went up for sale. The shop reminded me of the good times, and I wanted to be able to see where they happened every day."

He stroked my arm. "We can still go if you want to."

Shaking my head, I snuggled closer. "No, this is perfect. We can celebrate it there next year."

Time floated past as we lay together, lulled by the crackling fire and fragrant smoke.

We jerked when a log shifted, shooting sparks upward to be carried away by the breeze. The cold breeze. Growing colder by the minute.

When I shivered, Raider eased out from under me and pulled the blanket over us. We'd dressed warm for the predicted chilly forecast, prepared to wait out Samhain until dawn, but I still trembled when the breeze picked up and made its way down my collar.

He turned on his side and cupped my face, his midnight stare turning darker. Arrogant. Sexier. "Would you like me to warm you, love?" Not waiting for a reply, he grasped my nape and pulled me close. His lips were firm and warm. I opened for him, letting his mouth work its magic. But we'd perfected the ritual by then—he kissed me to the edge of release, but no further. He didn't like it, but I'd made it clear the next orgasm he gave me would be the old-fashioned way, which he refused to do until I was *healed*.

I moaned and swung a leg over his hip, grinding against his erection. Goddess, I was so close. And almost tempted to let it happen. But Raiden's head snapped back, and he pushed my leg back down.

"It's going to be a long night if we keep this up." He rolled away.

"Then don't stop."

He glanced at me from the corner of his eye and licked his lips.

I narrowed my gaze and said, "I'm not going to let you use my accident as an excuse anymore."

"You aren't?" The lust and hope on his face nearly made me laugh.

I sat up and unbuttoned my jacket, unzipped my

jeans, and slid them off, tossing them aside. Goose bumps rose over my bare skin, and I got back under the blanket. Raiden's mouth hung open and his unsteady breathing empowered me. "Your turn."

"You're really serious."

"I wouldn't risk frostbite if I wasn't." I unbuttoned his heavy wool pea coat and slipped my good hand under his flannel shirt. His skin was on fire, stretched tight over tensed abs.

He pushed my hand away and unzipped his jeans. Under the blanket, he slipped them over his hips, white puffs of breath escaping his mouth as he panted. His excitement fueled my own, and my core throbbed with impatience. We were well past the time to do exactly this, our bodies primed for the joining.

Rolling to his side again, he said, "I don't want to hurt you."

"I'll be fine, Raiden. I'm not a virgin."

He gave a short growl, as though that thought didn't bear consideration. As if he'd played the celibate card until he'd met me.

"I was talking about your arm, actually."

With a short laugh, I murmured against his mouth, "Worry about the important stuff." Not letting him protest any longer, I lay flat on my back and tugged him on top of me. His erection pressed against my thigh, and I bit back a groan.

I could not wait.

He braced one arm alongside my head and kissed me long and thoroughly. The other hand cupped one breast, finding the hard nipple and working it through my sweater. I writhed under him and tried to hook a leg around his to get what I wanted closer to where I wanted it.

"Easy, love. Patience is a virtue." He slid the hand lower and I jerked when it brushed across my belly. Every inch of my skin was sensitive to his touch.

It felt wonderful.

When his thumb found my clit, I hissed and tensed, trying to close my legs around his hand. "Please."

He continued to stroke. "Please what, Tamsin?"

"I want you inside me this time." I was blind

with lust. All I cared about was having him fill me. Burying my face in his neck, I moaned with the imminent release barreling toward me.

And with a slight shifting of his heavy body, he obeyed, spreading my legs wide with his knee. He entered me slowly, pushing and retreating, and I relished the pleasant burn. Finally. Finally we were one.

He straightened his arms and rose until only our lower bodies touched. Staring down at me, he said, "I have waited so long for you." And he began to move in a smooth glide, for a long while only letting the delicious friction linger without going further.

The wind shifted direction and settled, bringing the warmth and scent of the fire closer to us, warding off the bite in the air.

Raiden stopped and rested on his elbows. After one last long kiss, he moved again with shorter and quicker thrusts, his hips grinding into mine, hitting every erogenous zone at the same time.

Thunder rumbled and one of the heavier logs thudded in a shower of sparks.

I opened my eyes and found him staring back.

"Come for me, love." He pumped harder, driving into me.

More thunder. A crack of lightning. Our mouths met, tongues twisting in time with our bodies, and I splintered. Twisting my head away, I shrieked, arching into Raiden, letting the spasms carry me. He was relentless, driving into me until I sobbed for him to stop. On a final thrust, he came with a thunderous boom that shook the earth. Literally.

After we caught our breath, he rolled to his side, tugging me with him, taking care not to hurt my arm. He kissed me softly, as if sealing the moment, then his eyes fluttered shut. I watched him for several minutes, memorizing his features for the hundredth time, never tiring of him.

I hadn't realized I'd drifted into a satiated haze until what felt like pinpricks poked my face. Then my eyelids. Frowning, I squinted, peeking through the slits.

Snow.

It was snowing.

Like the vision I'd had. Sex, tangled limbs, snow, and all.

I began to laugh.

Raiden murmured, "What's so funny. And you'd better not say my name."

I raised my good arm and pointed. Fluffy flakes had begun to fall in earnest, coating the ground and hissing when they hit the bonfire. "Look."

Lifting his head, he glanced around then shrugged

I poked him in the ribs. "You know what this means?"

"Uh...it's snowing and we're naked?"

"That, and—" I planted a solid, possessive kiss on his lips, "Revenge is a dish best served cold."

Maia's Cheddar-Bacon Treats

1 cup rolled oats
1/3 cup bacon fat (or shortening, although Maia says the bacon stuff is sublime)
1 cup boiling water
3/4 cup cornmeal
2 teaspoons white sugar
2 teaspoons beef bouillon low-sodium granules
1/2 cup milk
1 cup shredded cheddar cheese
1 egg, beaten
3 cups whole-wheat flour

Combine oats, bacon fat and boiling water in a large bowl. Let stand for ten minutes.
Stir in cornmeal, sugar, beef bouillon granules, milk, cheese and beaten egg. Mix in whole-wheat flour, one cup at a time. The batter will be stiff.

Knead dough on floured surface, adding more flour as needed, until dough is no longer sticky. Roll out to one-half inch thickness. Cut with cookie cutters. Bob Barkery uses cat-shaped cutters.Place on greased cookie sheets, about an inch apart, and bake in 325-degree Fahrenheit oven for 35-45 minutes or until golden brown.

Freeze what you don't think you'll use within a few days. Maia said they'll taste funny if you don't.

~About the Author~

Valerie Mann is the superwoman every woman tries to be—mother of five attractive, successful children, vixen in and out of the bedroom, runway model fashionista, extreme gardener, and just recently crashed on bestseller lists as a romance author.

In real life, Valerie is the mother of five lovely, but ordinary children. Sure, she's a vixen in and out of the bedroom, which explains the herd of kids. The closest she gets to a runway is an airport, and while she thinks gardens of all sorts are wonderful, she figures that hobby can wait until retirement (if her knees last that long). And that crashing you heard was Valerie collapsing on the couch at the end of a very long day.

As for romance, she writes and likes to think she can tell an amazing tale of love or two. Her husband of nearly thirty years won't read her stories because they make him blush, but is content in the knowledge he's the inspiration for every one of them.

Valerie is co-owner of Decadent Publishing and Wizards in Publishing, a company providing editing and formatting services for independent authors and boutique publishers.

You can reach Valerie at:
ValerieMann09@yahoo.com